The Chapter Book

Adapted by Annie Auerbach

Based on the film *HOP*

Story by Cinco Paul & Ken Daurio

Screenplay by Cinco Paul & Ken Daurio

and Brian Lynch

Little, Brown and Company

New York Boston

Copyright © 2011 by Universal Studios Licensing LLLP. HOP: The Movie is a
trademark and copyright of Universal Studios. Licensed by Universal Studios
Licensing LLLP. All rights reserved.

Except as permitted under the U.S. Copyright Act of 1976, no part of this publication
may be reproduced, distributed, or transmitted in any form or by any means, or stored
in a database or retrieval system, without the prior written permission of the publisher.

Little, Brown and Company
Hachette Book Group
237 Park Avenue, New York, NY 10017
Visit our website at www.lb-kids.com

Little, Brown and Company is a division of Hachette Book Group, Inc.
The Little, Brown name and logo are trademarks of Hachette Book Group, Inc.

The publisher is not responsible for websites (or their content) that are not owned by
the publisher.

First Edition: February 2011

The characters and events portrayed in this book are fictitious. Any similarity
to real persons, living or dead, is coincidental and not intended by the author.

ISBN 978-0-316-12900-8

10 9 8 7 6 5 4 3 2 1

CWO

Printed in the United States of America

Prologue

Seven-year-old Fred O'Hare slept soundly in his race car–shaped bed. Suddenly, his eyes popped open. He looked at the clock: 5:45 AM. Fred jumped out of bed and rushed to the window. He made it just in time to see over a dozen yellow chicks fly by, pulling a large, purple and blue egg-shaped sleigh. After the sleigh glided to a landing in Fred's backyard, rabbits and chicks jumped out and hid colorful Easter eggs everywhere.

And then Fred saw him...the Bunny in Charge. The Grand Pooh-bah of Easter. *The* Easter Bunny. He was supervising some rabbits carrying an Easter basket filled with delicious candy.

Fred couldn't believe what he was seeing. He quickly grabbed his camera and darted out of his room, down the hallway, and out the back door. He raised his camera, ready to capture the Easter Bunny on film...but the backyard was empty. A large chocolate Easter bunny wrapped in purple foil sat on the doorstep. Puzzled and disappointed, Fred picked up the bunny and looked at it for a moment. Then he sighed and went back inside.

Chapter 1

Thump, thump, thump, thump. Thump, thump, thump, thump.

The sound of drums echoed through Rapa Nui, more commonly known as Easter Island. Ancient, giant statues of heads stood facing the ocean, and on one particular statue sat an adorable little bunny playing the bongos.

"E.B.! E.B.!"

The young bunny's father was calling from the bottom of the statue.

"EEEEEEE.B.!!!"

Finally, E.B. heard him over his drumming and looked down. "Hi, Dad," he said. E.B. hopped up and slid down the nose of the statue. He landed right in his father's arms.

"E.B., how'd you like to see where your father works?"

The little bunny's eyes lit up. "Oh boy, would I!" he exclaimed.

Then E.B.'s father pushed a button at the base of an enormous statue of a head. The mouth opened, and E.B. and his father stepped inside an egg-shaped elevator, which closed behind them.

When the elevator doors opened again, the pair found themselves entering an incredible candy factory filled with treats that were all centered on Easter. Huge conveyor belts carried malted eggs, candied almonds, and colorful jelly beans. Vats of pure, glistening milk chocolate tipped forward to fill myriad molds of bunnies, chicks, and eggs. Bunnies painted intricate designs on eggs, while chicks sculpted chocolate bunnies. There were even chicks on roller skates zipping from one station to another, making sure everything was perfect.

"Someday, this will all be yours," E.B.'s father told him.

"Wow!" exclaimed E.B.

"It's a lot of responsibility," began his father. "But don't worry. I'm going to train you."

A chick skated up and handed E.B. a notebook. Another one handed him a pen.

E.B.'s father led his son through the factory. "Let's begin with candy production. Chocolate bunnies, lollipops, caramel eggs, candied fruit—tell me, son, what's your favorite Easter candy?"

"I like lollipops," E.B. said with excitement. E.B.'s father gave him a lollipop.

"Do you know what my favorite Easter candy is? All of them!" said E.B.'s father.

They passed the marshmallow chicks machine. E.B. grabbed a marshmallow chick and ate it. Carlos, a live chick with a thick Chilean accent, ran over to E.B.

"Hey! Little bunny! We NEVER dip into our stock."

When his father turned around, E.B. smiled, his mouth full of marshmallow. E.B.'s father put his arm on E.B.'s shoulder. "E.B., this is my second in command, Carlos. It's fine, Carlos. E.B. was...taste testing. Isn't that right, son?"

E.B. smiled and gave a thumbs-up.

E.B.'s father tasted one of the chicks and spat it out.

"Oh dear, no. Carlos, too much marsh, not enough mallow," he said.

"*Sí, señor*," said Carlos. "I was just going to say that." He pointed to a tiny chick with a Mohawk.

"Phil! What do I always tell you? Too much marsh! Not enough mallow!"

A confused look crossed Phil's face. "You've never said that," he told Carlos.

E.B.'s father looked at his son. "You can't make mistakes, E.B. The magic and joy of Easter will rest solely on you."

E.B.'s shoulders sagged. This wasn't what he

wanted to do with his life. But his father didn't know that.

"You'll pick it up sooner or later," his father continued. He pointed to a golden scepter adorned with a red, shining egg. "Why, ten more years of this, and you'll be ready to pick up the Egg of Destiny and become the Easter Bunny!"

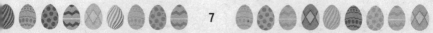

Chapter 2

Ten years later, E.B. still loved playing the drums but did not love the idea of becoming the next Easter Bunny. However, he did not stop his father from planning an elaborate ceremony to officially hand over the Egg of Destiny.

On the day of the coronation, E.B. was rocking out on his rabbit-size drum set in his room. He ended with a flourish and turned to his father, who was standing at the door.

"What do you think, Pop?"

E.B.'s father grimaced. "I think you're about to be crowned the Easter Bunny in front of three

thousand of your peers, and you should be rehearsing your speech!"

"Um, yeah, about that..." E.B. began, looking away from his father's gaze. "Look, Dad, I've been thinking. I don't know if Easter is my deal.

"Ever since I was yo-big," said E.B., "it's been 'The Easter Bunny wouldn't do that' and 'The Easter Bunny has to be perfect.' But I'm not perfect!"

He picked up a perfectly painted pink egg. "Maybe I'm not this," he continued, pointing to the egg.

E.B. scanned the room and picked up a sock. "Maybe I'm this."

"Maybe you're a sock?" asked his father.

"I might be a sock! I might not be a good-enough egg, but I might be the best sock ever! I might not cut it delivering eggs...." He pointed at the drums. "But I might be *great* at something else!"

"The drums?" his father said with a frown. "Great, so you have a hobby."

"It's not a hobby, Dad!" E.B. said. "I want to drum in a band. I want to see the world."

"The Easter Bunny *sees* the world," his father pointed out. "Every country in one night, making children of the world happy. For all those who believe, the Easter Bunny will be there. *You* will be there."

"No, Dad!" exclaimed E.B. "I don't *want* to be the Easter Bunny!"

"Four thousand years of tradition don't end just because one selfish bunny doesn't feel like doing it," said E.B.'s father.

Just before leaving the room, E.B.'s father turned, still clutching the sock, and added, "Remember, the measure of a man is in the choices he makes. I'll see you out there."

As night fell on Easter Island, the coronation ceremony began. E.B. walked glumly down the hallway toward his destiny as the next Easter Bunny. His father's words echoed in his head: "The measure of a man is in the choices he makes."

Then E.B. made a choice — his *own* choice. He darted around a corner and ran. Before long, he wriggled out of the nose of one of the biggest head statues. He pushed down on one stone, and a dark, swirling whirlpool appeared on the ground. It was a Rabbit Hole. Rabbit Holes were how the Easter Bunny traveled all over the world so quickly.

E.B. jumped into the hole, screaming as he flew into the vortex. There was a crackle of electricity, and then he was gone.

Phil was standing off to the side, chattering on his cell phone. He looked around at the noise and said, "Huh? Okay, whatever."

Into the phone, Phil said, "Yeah, they're doing the coronation. Nah, not allowed to go. I've got to guard the Rabbit Hole."

Chapter 3

It was dinnertime at the O'Hare house. Now in his late twenties, Fred still lived at home. Same bedroom. Same race car bed.

"Dinner!" his mother yelled from downstairs.

Fred joined his younger sister, Sam, at the table—she no longer lived at home, but she had stopped by for dinner. Their ten-year-old adopted sister, Alex, and their parents came in and sat around the dining room table.

"So...how are my kids doing?" Mr. O'Hare asked.

"I had rehearsals for the Easter play today," Alex said proudly. "They usually cast a boy as Peter Cottontail, but they made an exception for me because my singing voice is so strong."

"And Sam, how about you?" asked Mr. O'Hare.

"I'm up for a promotion at work," answered Sam.

Fred shifted uneasily in his chair. Something didn't seem right about the way his family was behaving.

Mr. O'Hare said, "It's so good to hear that two of my kids are working so hard. So, Fred...how'd the job interview go?"

Fred shrugged. "Not too sure about that place, Dad. I don't think it was what I was looking for."

"Did it pay money?" Mr. O'Hare asked. Fred nodded. "Then it's exactly what you've been looking for."

Mr. O'Hare looked at Alex and nodded at her. Alex nodded at Mrs. O'Hare, who, in turn, nodded at Sam.

Fred was puzzled. "Why are you nodding at each other? I want to be part of this. Dad, nod at me."

"Fred, we're concerned," said Mr. O'Hare. He and the others pulled out prepared statements.

"Fred, as your mother, I have always loved you," began Mrs. O'Hare.

"What is this, an intervention?" Fred asked, both amazed and horrified.

"We're doing this because we love you, Fred," explained Mr. O'Hare. "You need to get a life. You need to get a job, and you need to move out."

"I did move out!" Fred pointed out. "I had a job. Is it my fault the company downsized?"

"That was a year ago," Mr. O'Hare said. "You have to get back on the horse."

"You have so much potential," added Fred's mother.

Alex piped up. "Sometimes I think you adopted me because Fred was such a disappointment."

"Alex, that is a very hurtful statement," said Mr. O'Hare.

"You're not denying it," Alex said.

Fred ignored his sister and looked at his parents.

"Mom, Dad, I go on interviews. But you don't want me to settle, do you?"

"Settling would be fine," his mom replied quickly.

"Yes, please settle," his dad added.

"Of course you don't," Fred said, ignoring them. "When I was little, Dad, you said that when I grew up, I was going to do something great."

"And now I'm telling you that you should forget about 'great' and settle for getting *any* job," said Mr. O'Hare. "Baby birds get a nudge. Giant birds that leave the nest but then come back and never leave—they get shoved!"

Fred stood up. "Fine. I'll leave. Right now."

"Fred—" said his mother worriedly.

"No. Let him go," Mr. O'Hare said.

"It's fine," said Fred. "I *will* do something great. But I see now that I'm going to have to do it without any support from you guys. So thanks for nothing!"

"They raised you," Alex pointed out.

"Right, thank you for raising me," said Fred. "But other than that, thanks for nothing."

"We've given you a lot of money and a car," said Mr. O'Hare.

"Right," said Fred, softening even more. "Thank you for raising me and giving me all that money and the car—"

"And the love," added Sam.

"Good call," Fred said. "Thanks for raising me and giving me the money and the love and support and the car, but other than that..." He got back to his angry place again. "Thanks for nothing!"

Outside the front door, Fred sat down on the stoop, a duffel bag beside him. Sam walked out and sat next to him.

"Did you know about this, Sam?" Fred asked his sister.

"Look, the rules of the intervention state that I'm not supposed to help you," began Sam. Then she explained that she had gotten him a job interview the next day at her friend's video game company anyway.

"You know what? I'll swing by, if it means that much to you," Fred said casually.

"No, you won't 'swing by,'" Sam said forcefully. "You shower, you shave, you show up. You need to start your life. Think of this as a reboot."

"You're right," said Fred. "I can do this. In two weeks, you're going to see a whole new Fred. By Easter, there will be a new Fred. New job, new place, new life. This could be my finest hour!" He stood up to leave. "Now, if you'll excuse me, I'm going to go sleep in my car."

Sam rolled her eyes. "Fred, my boss is on vacation for a couple of weeks. He asked me to house-sit. He has dogs, and I'm scared of dogs. Take over for me." She handed him the keys. "But my boss loves his house more than he loves his kids," Sam warned. "So behave. Don't break anything. Don't touch anything. Do not go upstairs."

"Thanks, Sam," said Fred, hugging his sister.

They said good-bye, and Fred got in his car and drove away. He followed the directions Sam gave him and eventually found himself approaching an impressive mansion.

Outside, E.B. was looking up at the same mansion.

And then...car headlights shone in the bunny's eyes, brakes squealed, and...

THUNK!

Chapter 4

His ears askew, E.B. lay splayed out on the ground. He sat up and shook his head. He hadn't actually been hit. When E.B. saw the car door opening, he lay back down and pretended to be unconscious.

"No, no, no, no!" Fred said frantically. He examined his car. "My bumper!"

E.B. opened one eye and realized Fred wasn't concerned about the rabbit's condition. So he gave a long moan.

"Oh, man. It's alive," said Fred. "I've got to do something." He looked on the ground and picked

up a rock. "Don't worry, little friend, I will end your suffering."

"NO!" E.B. suddenly yelled, staring up at the rock.

Fred looked around. "Who said that?"

"I did," replied E.B.

A look of terror came over Fred's face as his eyes slid down to look at the talking rabbit. Fred's mouth fell open. And then he ran into the mansion— screaming. E.B. followed him all the way to the kitchen. Fred grabbed a pan for protection and said, "Say something. Talk again."

"Man, I am sooooo hungry," said E.B.

Fred gave the rabbit a carrot. "Now, time to hop away out of Fred's life, back to the Enchanted Forest."

"You're kicking me out?" said E.B.

"I'm sorry," replied Fred. "This is a really bad time."

E.B. crossed his arms. "Oh, did someone just hit you with his car? Is it that kind of a bad time?" He hopped down to the floor and pretended to limp to the front door. "No, it's fine. Ow! Ow! It's probably not broken in *too* many places."

Fred sighed. "Stop," he said. "On the off chance you are here and I did run you over and you are injured, I guess I should put you up."

E.B. brightened. "Really? Thanks, mate."

Fred set up some blankets and newspapers in the garage.

"What's this, then?" asked E.B. "I'm not a car. Why would I need to stay here?"

"I'm sorry," said Fred. "But even I'm not allowed to go upstairs, and I'm human." Then he went into the house, hoping that the whole "talking bunny thing" was just a dream.

Back on Easter Island, E.B.'s father walked through the factory. Whispers and rumors swirled around him.

The news that E.B. had gone through a Rabbit Hole finally reached the Easter Bunny.

E.B.'s father pulled out E.B.'s sock and squeezed it. "So he is gone," he said sadly. "Carlos, could I have handled the situation better?"

"Don't blame yourself," Carlos told him. "But we must find a way to move forward without him. Now that he's gone, who will make the Easter deliveries?"

"I guess I'll have to do it one more time," E.B.'s father said with a sigh.

That wasn't what Carlos wanted to hear. "*Señor*, with all due respect, taking into account your advanced age, shouldn't we begin looking for a replacement? It would have to be someone you trust, someone who's comfortable giving orders."

"You're right," agreed E.B.'s father.

"I'm totally right," Carlos said proudly. His moment had finally come! Carlos was about to be chosen as the new ambassador of Easter!

"We need to find E.B.!" declared E.B.'s father. "Carlos, assemble the Pink Berets."

Carlos was confused. *What just happened?* he thought.

"The Pink Berets?" he asked. "But they are only to be used in situations of extreme emergency!"

"This is pretty extreme, Carlos!" insisted E.B.'s father. "The Pink Berets will find E.B. They have to!"

Chapter 5

The next morning, Fred woke up and immediately checked the mansion for any signs of the rabbit.

"Talking rabbit? Helloooo?" he called out.

When there was no response, Fred breathed a huge sigh of relief. He must have imagined it. So he showered, brushed his teeth, and got dressed for his interview. And then he remembered...

"That's right, the dogs," he groaned. He was house-sitting for his sister's boss—and he had to feed the dogs! Well, it couldn't be that hard, right? He read the instructions taped to the dog food bag:

Until Daisy and Baby are accustomed to you, please wear the safety suit in the hall closet when you feed them.

Fred felt a little nervous. Why would he need a safety suit? But he put on the enormous padded suit anyway and went outside to feed the cute little dogs. Except they weren't cute little dogs—they were huge Rottweilers. They snarled and then charged right at Fred, taking him down.

A few minutes later, Fred retreated to the safety of the mansion. He slammed the door and locked it. The padded suit was now in shreds.

"It's fine, it's okay," Fred tried to reassure himself. Then he felt a drop of water on his shoulder. Puzzled, he looked up at the ceiling. Loud music blared from upstairs. Fred dashed to the second floor, horrified to see the stairs littered with half-eaten carrots.

"No, no, no!" he cried. He ran down the hall and opened a door to see E.B. playing the drums in a video game.

"You're still here!" Fred shouted at the bunny. "And you're in a forbidden part of the house!"

"Ah, but so are you," E.B. replied calmly. "I needed a soft bed."

"But your injury, your leg!" said Fred. "You climbed a flight of stairs?"

"*Struggled* up each stair is more like it," explained E.B. "It was worth it, too. The hot tub loosened me up."

"Hot tub?" Fred gasped. Wet rabbit footprints led into the bathroom. He ran in and saw the water still running in the big bathtub, overflowing onto the floor.

"No!" cried Fred, turning the water off. "Sam's going to kill me!"

Before E.B. knew it, he found himself in a box with a few holes punched in the side so he could breathe. Fred drove up to a trail in Runyon Canyon and got out of the car.

"Are we going for a hike?" E.B. asked from the box.

"Better," said Fred. "We're releas wild." He opened the box and trie out. But E.B. clung to the side.

"You're going to leave me here?" cried E.B. "But I talk!"

"Yes," Fred replied, turning the box upside down trying to get the rabbit out. "And you don't listen. I'm telling you: Go away!"

Fred smacked the side of the box, and E.B. fell to the ground.

"No, please! I'll behave!" the bunny begged as Fred began walking back to the car.

E.B. looked around him. He saw a sign labeled BEWARE OF RATTLESNAKES. He saw a man walking a fierce-looking pair of dogs. This was not where he belonged. He ran after Fred.

"But I'm special!" he pleaded.

"Yes, we're all special. Good-bye," said Fred. He opened his car door and got in.

E.B. hopped on the hood. "Fred, wait. You're not getting it. I mean I'm really special. Look!" He squatted and pooped out a pile of jelly beans.

"Ew," said Fred. He wasn't convinced.

So E.B. leaned in through the window and told "I'm the Easter Bunny!"

In an instant, Fred's car zoomed off, sending E.B. to the ground. Suddenly, the car screeched to a halt, then backed up. The car door opened.

"Say that again," Fred said to E.B.

"I'm the Easter Bunny," replied E.B.

"Hop in," said Fred.

As they drove, Fred was somewhat confused, but happy with this discovery. "I knew it! I knew you were real!"

"Of course I'm real," E.B. said.

"No, when I was little, I saw you on Easter morning. That was you, right?" asked Fred.

"Totally. Absolutely," lied E.B. He wasn't about to tell Fred that it was really his father who was the Easter Bunny.

"So, why are you here now?" asked Fred.

"Oh, I wish I could tell you, but that's top secret Easter business," explained E.B. "Very hush-hush."

Fred parked the car outside the office building where his interview was to take place. He turned to E.B. and said, "I have to do this job interview, and I don't think a normal human brain could handle seeing you. So do me this one favor and sit here until I get back. And *be good*!"

E.B. smiled sweetly. "I don't know any other way to be!" he told Fred.

Of course, the minute Fred was out of sight, E.B. started goofing around. He smushed his face against the windshield and made funny faces. Until...

"Oh, no," E.B. said gravely. He leaned forward to get a better look.

Hazy in the distance but coming closer were... the Pink Berets!

Chapter 6

The Pink Berets were an elite strike force called in by the Easter Bunny to help in extreme situations. E.B. on the run qualified as an extreme situation.

The bunnies meant business, and they wore pink berets to prove it. E.B. knew not to mess with those female rabbits. They knew karate, and they knew how to stun an enemy with just a jelly bean.

E.B. leaped for the car window and squeezed out through the small crack Fred had left for air. He hurriedly hopped toward the office building. Before long, he found Fred sitting in a chair, waiting to be called in for his interview.

"So when I asked you to stay in the car, there was some confusion?" Fred whispered.

"No, mate, you've got to help me—" began E.B.

"E.B., you can't be here!" insisted Fred. He didn't want the bunny to ruin his chances at this job. Fred pushed E.B. off the chair and into the trash basket just as he was called in for his interview.

E.B. popped out of the trash basket and turned toward the window. He saw the Pink Berets looking in cars, making their way to the office building. E.B. hopped out of the basket and tried to get Fred's attention. But it didn't work. So the bunny hurried down a hallway and then came to a stop.

The most incredible music was coming from a nearby room. E.B. opened the door and peeked in. Sitting on a small recording stage were the Blind Boys of Alabama. They were playing a blues song.

"Soundin' good to me," said one of them. "Where's Ricky? Let's throw a backbeat behind it."

E.B. was so excited he could hardly contain himself. "A backbeat? Wow!" he said to himself.

"Ricky went out for some coffee," another band member said as they all continued to play.

E.B. worked his way over to the drum set and took a seat. He began to play along.

"Well, I guess he's back," said the singer.

As E.B. continued drumming, things really began to heat up. Just outside the room, a woman was showing Fred around the office.

"This is our sound recording studio for our music games. We're doing *Extreme Blues Master*," the woman explained.

Fred looked in the window to the studio and saw E.B. playing the drums. Horrified, Fred waved frantically at E.B. But the bunny wasn't about to stop drumming!

When the song ended, E.B. said, "That was brilliant. Uh, I mean, outta sight!"

One of the Blind Boys spoke up. "Hey, I *know* that sounded all right. But I also know my own drummer when I hear him. Who are you, boy?"

"All right. You caught me, fellas," E.B. said

sheepishly. "I'm E.B. Just some guy off the street with two sticks of wood and a dream. I understand if you throw me out. I get it if you don't want to give me a break—"

"Hey, slow the tempo a little, friend," said a bandmate. "I got a buddy who's always on the lookout for new talent. Man's a genius. He's the godfather of entertainment." He held out a pamphlet. "He's holding auditions tomorrow."

E.B. took the pamphlet and read it: *Open Auditions for* We Know Talent, *a live television competition hosted and judged by a former actor-turned-musician.* "Wow!" E.B. exclaimed. "You think he can help me?"

"*If* he likes you," said one of the guys.

"Thanks, Blind Boys," said E.B.

"Good luck, little rabbit," one of the Blind Boys replied.

E.B. paused. "Wait. How did you know I was—"

The Blind Boys all grinned at him.

E.B. smiled. "Clever gents," he said. He left the room, clutching the pamphlet tightly in his hand.

When E.B. saw Fred, he turned tail and ran the

other way. Fred looked really angry, and he lunged after E.B. He finally cornered E.B. in a cubicle. Fred smashed into the cubicle, taking down the desk, the computer, and everything else, trying to catch the wiggly rabbit.

When Fred paused from chasing E.B. and saw the mess he'd made, he knew it was pretty clear that he didn't get the job.

Chapter 7

Back in his car, Fred was furious at E.B. "This is what the Easter Bunny does now? Goes from house to house, messing up people's lives?"

"Well, that's just hurtful," replied E.B.

"You tanked my interview!" Fred exclaimed.

E.B. looked over. "Fred, you're the one who went completely psycho in there. Besides, you're selling yourself short. They were going to shove you in the mailroom. Well, excuse me, but I happen to think you're better than that."

"You don't know me! We just met!" said Fred.

"Fred, I'm serious," said E.B. "You're destined to do something great. I just know it."

While Fred considered this idea, E.B. plunged ahead. "As for me, I have a date with destiny. And a drum set. And I will achieve this dream via the help of two men." He nodded at Fred to indicate he was one of the men, and he handed him the *We Know Talent* pamphlet to clue him in on the other.

"No," Fred said.

"Come on, man," begged E.B. "You drive me to the audition, and I'll get out of your life."

Fred thought this was the best news he'd heard all day. "Just one problem," he said. "You can't talk."

"No, I can. It's part of my package," said E.B.

"But you shouldn't. People will freak out," explained Fred.

Just as he pulled the car up to the mansion, Fred slammed on the brakes.

"Uh-oh, my sister's here!" he said worriedly. He thought about the damage E.B. had done upstairs and the flood in the bathroom. "If she goes upstairs, I'm dead."

Fred warned E.B. to stay quiet. "You sneak upstairs and clean up."

"Roger that!" E.B. said, and hopped out.

Fred walked inside the mansion and found Sam.

"So, how'd the interview go?" she asked.

"Aced it. Yeah, for sure," began Fred. "Place could use me, too. I mean, don't get me wrong, it's great. Well, not sure it was the best fit. Yeah...I didn't get it."

"Oh, Fred." Sam sighed.

"I know, I know," Fred replied, hanging his head.

Just then, they heard a noise from upstairs.

"What was that?" asked Sam.

"The pipes in this old place—" started Fred.

"Make the pitter-patter of tiny feet?" finished Sam. She wasn't buying it.

"I couldn't say, because I'm not allowed to go upstairs," said Fred. "And neither are you!"

But Sam was already halfway up the stairs. She headed into the master bedroom. "Oh my god!"

"Sam, I can explain!" said Fred. He caught up with her. But the bedroom and bathroom looked perfect. E.B. sat motionless on the bed.

"Look how cute that stuffed bunny is!" Sam cooed as she picked him up. "It's so lifelike."

"You think so?" asked Fred. "It's kind of freakish looking."

Sam hugged the bunny and then spotted a pile of jelly beans on the desk.

"No!" Fred said, trying to stop her. "You don't know where they've been...and I do."

"Relax, Fred," said Sam, popping a jelly bean into her mouth. "Mmm...cotton candy."

Fred cringed and then followed Sam down the stairs and to the front door. Before she left, she reminded Fred about their little sister's play the following night.

"I'm not going," said Fred.

"You have to go," insisted Sam. "It's your sister. Dress nice and be there at seven."

"Uh-huh. Bye, Sam," said Fred, closing the door.

E.B. hopped down and joined Fred. "That was close!" said the bunny. Then he added, "Is she seeing anyone?"

Fred glared at the bunny. It had been a very long day.

Chapter 8

A long line stretched around the theater where the *We Know Talent* auditions were taking place. There were dance crews, dog acts, jugglers, and more. In the middle of the line stood Fred, with E.B. safely tucked away in Fred's backpack. E.B. poked his head out, and his ears started trembling.

"Are you nervous?" Fred asked him.

"No, what's there to be nervous about?" E.B. replied defensively. "It's just the…the man who makes or breaks careers with one arch of his eyebrow. Can we go? I can't do it. Let's go!"

"Come on," Fred said, trying to calm him down. "This is your big opportunity."

"But what if they think I'm weird?" asked E.B.

"You *are* weird," Fred said without hesitating. "Don't worry. I'll give you a great intro. You'll be fine."

"Yeah? Really?" said E.B. "Thanks, Fred."

"No problem," said Fred. "Now please remove your claws from my back!"

The line moved slowly, but eventually, it was E.B.'s turn. Fred took the stage and put the backpack on the ground.

"I know you've seen it all," he said to the judge. "But this will stretch the limits of even *your* vast experience."

"Cut to the chase, friend," the actor-turned-musician said, running his fingers through his thick, wavy hair.

"Oh, okay," Fred said timidly. "Here's E.B."

E.B. popped out and then hopped to the drums. He nervously climbed to the drum stool and picked up the drumsticks. *Bam, bam, bam.* E.B. started playing. Before long, the bass player and guitar player joined in. E.B. let loose, and he sounded great.

"Stop, stop, stop!" the judge shouted. "I don't want to hear any more."

E.B. stopped playing.

"We've been waiting here all day. Give him a chance," Fred pleaded.

"I gave him a chance," replied the actor. "But I didn't like it... I *loved* it! I know talent, and this rabbit's got it!"

"Woooooo-hooooo! Yes!" cheered E.B. "Thank you! You have no idea how wonderful that—"

Suddenly E.B. realized that he had talked in front of another human. He slapped his hand over his mouth. He looked at Fred.

The Hollywood star waited a moment and then said, "Okay, cool. Can you make it to a live taping of the show next Saturday night? I'll send a limo."

"Wait. You're not freaked out that I'm a talking rabbit?" asked E.B.

The judge just smiled.

"Did you hear him? I'm on my way, Fred!" E.B. cheered once they were outside.

"He really acted like he dug you," said Fred. "I mean, he's a good actor, but I think it was genuine."

"Thanks, mate," said E.B. "And don't think I've forgotten our deal. You've done your part. I'm ready to get out of your life. But we've had some good times, huh?"

"There were some moments in there," said Fred.

Fred turned and realized E.B. was gone. He found the rabbit hiding behind a car.

"Pink Berets!" E.B. said, pointing.

Fred looked around. "There's nobody there."

"Oh yes, there is. Trust me," said E.B. "If they see me, I have to go back to Easter Island."

"Wow. Pink Berets. They sound super-fearsome," joked Fred.

"Don't be fooled by their adorable name," E.B. said seriously. "They're the Easter Bunny's royal guard."

"But *you're* the Easter Bunny," said Fred. "Aren't you?"

"Of course I am," said E.B. Then he added quietly, "Technically. I was supposed to take over this year. I ran away."

They got in Fred's car. E.B. sat low on the seat, hiding.

"Who wouldn't want to be the Easter Bunny? It's the coolest job ever!" said Fred.

"Not when your dad drills it into your head day after day. Always droning on about growing up and responsibility."

Fred nodded. "Sometimes fathers just don't get it."

E.B. told Fred what his father always said: "E.B., you only think about yourself."

Fred thought that was exactly right! "You *are* selfish, E.B."

E.B. started sniffling. "I can't go back to Easter Island, and *you* don't want me, and I was so close to achieving my dream!"

"What do you want me to do?" Fred asked. "I

can't leave you anywhere, and I have to get to my sister's play."

"I like plays," E.B. said, a tear running down his cheek.

"Argh!" said Fred. "You are by far the most manipulative rabbit I have ever met!"

Chapter 9

At the elementary school, Fred arrived in a nice suit and carried a briefcase. He sat next to his parents and Sam. When the performance began, Alex took center stage to sing a song about the Easter Bunny.

Alex's singing was so bad that E.B. peeked out of the briefcase to take a look. That's when he hopped on Fred's shoulder and yelled, "Run for it! It's the Pink Berets!"

Alex stopped singing. The audience fell silent.

E.B. looked around and realized that who he thought were the Pink Berets were actually just three little kids in bunny costumes. "Never mind,

everyone! False alarm," said E.B. "Continue with your awful singing."

"How did that rabbit just talk?" Mr. O'Hare wondered aloud.

"He's been studying ventriloquism," E.B. answered.

At that, Fred slid his hand up the back of E.B.'s shirt and pretended to throw his voice.

"Fred, stop making a fool of yourself!" demanded his father.

"Why should he?" E.B. answered. Then he made Fred get up onstage. "I hope that with all this fanfare and dressing up, we haven't forgotten the *true* meaning of Easter—candy!"

E.B. cleared his throat and began singing. The kids and audience loved it and happily joined in.

Afterward, Fred found Alex. "Great job tonight," he told her.

She kicked him in the shins. Alex couldn't believe he had stolen her spotlight.

Then Fred's father found him. "Is this your new career? Upstaging grade-schoolers with your ventriloquist puppet?"

Fred noticed a distinct look on his father's face.

"There it is," said Fred.

"What?" asked Mr. O'Hare.

"That look. Complete and utter disappointment," explained Fred.

"I'm sorry, Fred," said his father. "But can you give me just, I don't know, one reason to *not* be disappointed?"

"I...well...uh..." Fred looked around nervously. He glanced down at the briefcase and had an idea. "I do have a pretty solid lead. A great job, actually."

His father wasn't convinced. "Uh-huh."

"Yeah, I don't want to jinx it before the final offer comes in, so you'll have to wait," said Fred. "But it's big—really big!"

Back at the mansion, E.B. and Fred sat at the kitchen table. Fred took a deep breath and looked E.B. in the eye.

"So, E.B., when I was a kid, I told everyone I saw

the Easter Bunny. Nobody believed me. That did a number, let me tell you," he said. "But tonight I realized that it was my destiny to see him, just like it was my destiny to meet you. It's all been building up to this!"

"Up to what?" asked E.B.

"You don't want to be the Easter Bunny," Fred pointed out. "I know who can take your place: me."

E.B. slapped him.

"What was that for?" cried Fred.

"That's for people who have gone loony," explained E.B. "A *human* Easter Bunny? That makes no sense."

"A *bunny* makes no sense! You deliver eggs! If we're bringing logic into this, it should be an Easter Chicken!" Fred pointed out. "You said I was destined for great things."

"Yes, but I meant that more as a way to distract you from blaming me for ruining your interview," E.B. admitted.

"I don't care," said Fred. "If you can be a drummer, I can be the Easter Bunny."

E.B. sighed. "You can't just *be* the Easter Bunny. It takes years of egg-painting classes. Plus, the Easter Bunny's got to be fit. You're a little flabby. The Easter Bunny's bottom has to be spring-loaded for hopping and maximum speed."

But Fred was determined. "I will *be* the Easter Bunny. I'll show you I can do it!"

Chapter 10

On Easter Island, things were not going well. E.B.'s father kept falling asleep in front of the candy-making machines.

Off to the side, Carlos whispered to Phil and the other chick workers. "Look at the old man. Feeble, stubborn. He refuses to crown anyone else—which means we're going to have to take matters into our own hands."

Phil raised a wing. "We don't have hands."

Carlos clenched his teeth. "Figure of speech, Phil," he said. "Too long have we labored under the

yolk of the bunnies' tyranny. Well, no more! It's time for the Easter Chick to rise."

Every chick raised a wing.

"So, who's going to run the show, make deliveries, be the man?" asked Phil.

"Who do you *think* is going to do it?" Carlos said, annoyed.

Phil looked hopeful. "Is it me?"

Carlos glared at him. "No, Phil. It's *me*." Then he ordered the chicks back to work...for now.

Meanwhile, Fred was taking his Easter Bunny training very seriously. He wanted to prove to E.B. that he could do the job.

First, Fred painted hundreds of eggs.

Then, he grabbed an Easter basket and bounced on a trampoline.

"Hey, E.B., check it out!" called Fred. "I'm hopping almost as high as you do! Watch, I'll do a flip."

"I wouldn't..." said E.B., looking doubtful.

Fred tried to flip, bounced off the trampoline, and hit the ground.

E.B. didn't say "I told you so," but he was definitely thinking it.

Next, Fred sprinted around the backyard, clutching a basket filled with eggs.

"Easter Bunny's got to be fast," Fred said to E.B.

"You're not fast—at all," said E.B. "What you need is motivation." So E.B. released the Rottweilers. Daisy and Baby immediately sprinted after Fred, who ran for his life.

"Aaaaahh!" screamed Fred.

"Better," said E.B., nodding. "Don't drop any eggs!"

After many more hours of practice, Fred soon was able to paint eggs while blindfolded. He became smarter and quicker than the dogs. Holding an egg, he would jump high into the air, grab a tree branch, and pull himself to safety. Even E.B. was impressed by *that* move.

When Fred felt he was ready, there was one thing left for him to do: tell his family about his new job.

The only problem was that no one believed him. His parents and his sisters thought he had gone completely nuts.

"I am training to be the Easter Bunny," he explained.

"At a mall?" asked his father.

"No, I'm training to be the actual Easter Bunny," Fred replied. "Is this really that difficult to believe?"

No one said a word.

Fred sighed. "This is not how I wanted this to go." Then he added, "I'm just so sick of seeing that disappointed look on your faces. I wanted to get that other look, the one you give Sam and Alex. What's that called?"

"Pride?" suggested Alex.

"Exactly," said Fred. "I just wanted to make you proud."

As Fred looked at the disappointed faces of his family, he felt extremely sad. They didn't believe him, and they certainly didn't feel proud.

"I should go," he said quietly, and left.

When Fred walked in through the door of the mansion, E.B. was drumming along to a music video.

"So, how was dinner? What'd you bring me?" asked the rabbit.

"Well, great news, for starters," said Fred. "I've officially replaced my late aunt Joanna as the crazy person in the family. She left all her money to her pet hamster."

"What's crazy about that?" asked E.B.

"I don't know what I was thinking," Fred continued. "They thought I was nuts. They're right, aren't they? I can't be the Easter Bunny, can I?"

"Well, you tried...." E.B. said.

Fred's shoulders slumped.

"You don't want the job anyway," E.B. told him. "The pressure is horrible."

"Why didn't you tell me how stupid I was being?" asked Fred.

"I didn't want to jelly bean on your dreams," replied E.B.

"No!" Fred said angrily. "You led me on. You're an Easter tease. Oh, anything goes, so long as drummer boy gets his big dream! I wish I had run over a non-magical rabbit who didn't think only about himself!"

Fred slammed the door, and E.B. stormed away.

The next morning, E.B. woke up on the couch, a noise stirring him from sleep. He saw three rabbit shadows move across the wall. He leaped up and looked outside—the limo to his audition was waiting, but he knew those shadows belonged to the Pink Berets. He quickly came up with a plan, set it in motion, then snuck outside to catch the limo to his *We Know Talent* appearance.

The Pink Berets were in the backyard, creeping quietly past the sleeping Rottweilers. The rabbits dropped through the mail slot on the front door and made their way to the kitchen. One of them spotted a pot on the stove. The leader removed the lid and pulled out a boiled chicken that was wearing

E.B.'s clothes. They immediately thought Fred had killed E.B.!

Just then, Fred opened the door from his room and headed down the hallway to the kitchen.

"Whoa," he said when he saw the three bunnies. "Wait! I know who you are. You're the Pink Berets. E.B. said you were so scary, but you're so cute."

One of the rabbits took out a blow-dart and fired it at Fred's neck. He collapsed immediately. As the Pink Berets dragged the unconscious Fred out of the house, E.B. watched from the limo.

"He'll be fine," E.B. said to himself.

But would he be?

Chapter 11

"**E**aster Island. I knew it!" Fred said excitedly after he opened his eyes. He looked around the Easter factory with glee.

Then he tried to move and realized that he was tied to a piece of machinery.

"Murderer!" shouted Carlos. He spit at Fred's feet.

"I'm picking up a little tension in the room," Fred said.

"Carlos, let me handle this," said E.B.'s father.

Fred's eyes widened as he saw *the* Easter Bunny

standing before him. "You're him. Wow. I'm Fred O'Hare. We met once—it's been a while. I don't expect you to remember me."

Carlos piped up again. "What is wrong with you—killing a defenseless rabbit? What did E.B. ever do to you?"

"Did you say *kill*?" exclaimed Fred. "I didn't kill E.B. He's my friend!"

"*Lies!*" Carlos yelled.

E.B.'s father asked the Pink Berets to explain what they saw in bunny speak. The bunnies described finding the boiled chicken wearing E.B.'s clothes. They pantomimed it as they squeaked, so Fred could tell they were giving the wrong impression.

"Wait a minute, that's not—" began Fred.

"So it's true. My son is...dead," said E.B.'s father, his eyes filling with tears. He asked Carlos to bring him his darkest green vest as a sign of mourning. "I can't even think about Easter after this heavy, heavy blow."

"We wouldn't expect you to, sir," Carlos said quickly. "I will handle everything." He picked up a megaphone and ordered all the bunnies to report to the egg-painting room.

All the bunnies, except for E.B.'s father and the Pink Berets, filed into the egg-painting room. Then Carlos closed the door and locked them in! The chicks surrounded E.B.'s father.

"Carlos, what's going on?"

"It's called a coup d'etat," said Carlos. "Which is French for *coup d'etat*."

It was a revolt! Carlos and the chicks were taking over the factory!

The Pink Berets stepped forward and created a bunny shield around E.B.'s father. Carlos, who was holding a nozzle attached to a hose, fired a stream of liquid chocolate at the Pink Berets. The chocolate immediately hardened, leaving them frozen in awesome karate positions.

"I don't understand," E.B.'s father said. "You've been my most trusted number two for years."

"I am sick of doing number two!" cried Carlos. "It is our time for number one. Sorry, old man. You will pick up the Egg of Destiny, and you will crown *me* the Easter Chick!"

"I will do no such thing!" insisted E.B.'s father.

Carlos smiled wickedly. "I was hoping you'd say that. Seize him!"

Meanwhile, E.B. sat in a dressing room at the studio where they were filming *We Know Talent*. He was depressed.

Before long, it was time to perform. He walked down a long hall toward the stage. E.B. realized it felt very similar to the time he was almost crowned the Easter Bunny. He heard his father's words in his head: "The measure of a man is in the choices he makes."

E.B. stopped. Was he making a mistake?

Just then, the famous actor-turned-musician approached him. "How's my little guy?"

"Actually, there's a problem," said E.B. "This drumming thing is for myself. But meanwhile, I'll be letting a lot of people down if I don't go right now. I just let my friend take the rap for murder. I have to clear his name."

The star put his hand on E.B.'s shoulder and said, "Go to him."

"This is your last chance...." Carlos warned.

The Easter Bunny hung suspended by a crane over a vat of boiling pink egg dye. But he remained firm in his belief. "I will never turn Easter over to you. Never!"

Carlos flipped a lever, and the crane began lowering E.B.'s father toward the bubbling pink dye.

"Tonight, the bunnies' reign is over!" declared Carlos.

Suddenly, E.B. popped up next to Fred. The bunny pulled Fred out of view and untied him.

"E.B., you came!" exclaimed Fred.

"Shhhh!" warned E.B. "Of course I did. We're mates." He took a look around. "But I'm going to need your help, if you want to become the Easter Bunny."

Fred grinned. "Seriously? Okay! I'll distract them. You save your dad."

Fred jumped up and yelled, "Hey, chicks! How'd I escape? Weird, huh?" Fred ran for it, and the chicks quickly chased after him.

At the same time, E.B. stopped the crane from lowering his father any closer to the boiling dye. "Sorry, Carlos. Boiled bunny is off the menu."

Carlos turned to see E.B. So did E.B.'s father, who was overcome with joy. His son was alive!

A group of chicks rushed E.B., who hopped out of danger. But that left the lever unguarded.

"I decide what's on the menu!" said Carlos, flipping the lever on again.

At the same time, Fred used his new Easter Bunny training to hop high into the air. He landed on a turret that had a marshmallow injector. From his perch, Fred began taking out chicks below with globs of sticky marshmallow.

Carlos and E.B. started battling on a conveyor belt. Each second they fought, E.B.'s father was a second closer to becoming a boiled bunny. E.B. had to save him. The bunny hopped up to a crank for the gum ball machine. Carlos sent a blast of liquid chocolate up at E.B., but the rabbit leaped out of the way. The chocolate blast turned the crank— triggering an avalanche of gum balls that buried Carlos!

E.B. ran for the crane lever and turned it off. His father was safe.

But the chicks were still on a mission. "Get E.B.! For the glory of Carlos!" The chicks rushed at E.B., until Fred yelled, "*Stop!*"

The entire factory floor of chicks froze in silence.

"What are you doing? We're wasting time," Fred continued. "It's Easter eve!"

The chicks looked at him.

"He's right," agreed E.B. "We can keep fighting or we can put this ugliness behind us and bring happiness to children all over the world. The choice is yours."

Without wasting another moment, the chicks ran around, manning their stations. They released all the bunny workers from the egg-painting room. Even Carlos popped out of the gum balls and helped out. It was time to get ready for Easter!

E.B. untied his father, and they hugged.

"Thank you, son. I'm so glad you came back."

"Me, too," said E.B.

"But you don't have to be the Easter Bunny if you don't want to," said his father. "For years, I've put Easter ahead of my own boy. This whole incident has made me think. You should follow your dream." He pulled E.B.'s sock out of his pocket. "You want to be a sock? You go be the best sock ever."

E.B. was touched by his father's offer, but he had a better idea. "I can play drums *and* be the Easter Bunny."

Then he introduced his father to Fred. E.B.'s father picked up the Egg of Destiny and walked up to Fred.

Fred brightened. "Does this mean . . . ?"

E.B. nodded. "Come on, Fred. Let's do something great."

Chapter 12

The egg sleigh rocketed away from Easter Island. E.B. sat behind the wheel, with Fred next to him. They flew over the Eiffel Tower, the Taj Mahal, and all the points in between. It was the greatest night of Fred's life.

Sometime later, Fred's family hosted a party in their backyard. E.B., his father, the Pink Berets, and all the chicks and bunnies were invited.

E.B.'s father approached Mr. O'Hare. The rabbit held out his hand.

Mr. O'Hare was taken aback. "It's an honor, sir," he said, shaking the rabbit's hand.

"I heard you had to throw your son out of your house," E.B.'s father said.

Mr. O'Hare nodded. "Felt like he needed a kick in the pants."

E.B.'s father smiled. "Well, it's a good thing. He helped save Easter."

Fred's father beamed and then turned to smile at Fred.

Across the yard, Fred looked at his father. "Hey, E.B., is that...?"

"Oh yes, mate," said E.B. "That's pride."

Fred smiled back at his father. He had finally made his dad proud!

Then he looked at his new friend and fist-bumped E.B.'s paw. "Grab your drumsticks," he told him, "and get a beat going."

"Let's hop!"